# G. ... Teeth

by
## David Webb

First published
April 07 in Great Britain by

PUBLISHING

ISBN-10 1-905637-20-9
ISBN-13 978-1-905637-20-1

Educational Printing Services Limited
Albion Mill, Water Street, Great Harwood, Blackburn BB6 7QR
Telephone: (01254) 882080          Fax: (01254) 882010
E-mail: enquiries@eprint.co.uk          Website: www.eprint.co.uk

# Contents

# Chapter 1
# The Missing Teeth

'I can't find m' teeth!' shouted
Grandma, flinging the cushions off the sofa.
'You haven't seen them anywhere, have you,
Dudley?'

'No, Grandma,' sighed Dudley, wearily.
'It was your glasses yesterday. Remember?

1

You couldn't find your glasses. They were in the washing machine.'

'That wasn't my fault,' said Grandma, quickly. She sucked her gums and scratched her thinning grey hair. 'I left them wrapped up in a tea towel and your mother put it in the washing machine.'

Grandma's lips smacked together like two wet fish every time she spoke.

'Just stop and think for a minute,' urged Dudley, as another cushion flew through the air and landed on the television. 'You've probably put them somewhere safe.'

Grandma scratched her head again and blinked her beady little eyes.

'That'll be it!' she exclaimed, hopping from one foot to the other. 'I've put them somewhere safe!' She looked puzzled for a few seconds and then she said: 'Where have I put them, Dudley?'

It was the half term holiday and Dudley had been looking forward to a good rest. He had forgotten that Grandma was coming to stay for the week and now he was already wishing that he was back at school.

At that moment, Dudley's mum rushed into the room and glanced around in panic.

'Dudley!' she exclaimed, angrily. 'Have you been throwing cushions around again? You really should know better at your age!'

'But.... but....' began Dudley.

'No buts,' interrupted Mum. 'I'm late for work and I can't find my car keys. Has anyone seen them?'

'They're probably with Grandma's teeth,' muttered Dudley, under his breath.

'It's no good,' sighed Mum, looking totally flustered. 'I'll have to catch the bus again. Now, you make sure you tidy this room up, Dudley. Bye!'

And with that, she flew out of the room, banging the door closed behind her.

Dudley shook his head in dismay. He just knew that the day was going to be a disaster.

'I've got them!' shouted Grandma.

Dudley turned to see Grandma crouching on the floor on all fours with her arm stuck underneath the couch.

'How on earth did your teeth get under there?' asked Dudley.

'I've not found m' teeth, you silly boy, I've found your mother's keys!'

Grandma pulled out her wrinkled arm and waved the keys in the air.

'That's very good,' said Dudley, forcing a weak smile, 'but what are we going to do about your teeth, Grandma?'

'Well, as it happens,' began Grandma, slowly, 'I've ordered a new set from the dentist. There's only one thing for it, Dudley – you'll have to take me to the dentist.'

Dudley's blood ran cold. The colour drained from his face and his hands began to shake.

'Take you to the dentist....' he repeated, quietly. He remembered the absolute chaos Grandma had caused last time he had taken her out. He could still picture the fireman's face as he carried her out of the burning supermarket.

'That's right,' grinned Grandma, with an evil glint in her eyes, 'you'll have to take me to the dentist.'

Dudley put his hands together, raised his eyes towards heaven and mouthed a silent prayer.

## Chapter 2
## The Dentist's Surgery

Mr Bernard Brace, the dentist, moved the phone away from his ear slowly as his bottom lip began to tremble with shock.

'Whatever is the matter?' asked Rose, his attractive young assistant.

Rose was concerned. Mr Brace was usually so confident.

'It's that dratted woman,' hissed the dentist, wiping a bead of sweat from his forehead. 'You know? – Dudley Duckworth's grandma. She's in the waiting room.'

Mr Brace sat down and took a deep breath. 'She almost wrecked the surgery last time she came and she was only here to get fitted for a new set of false teeth!'

'I remember,' said Rose, the smile disappearing from her normally cheerful face. 'She kept whizzing up and down on your chair. You had to force her fingers off the lever in the end.'

'That's the one,' said the troubled dentist, nodding his head, slowly. 'And then she spat mouthwash all over the floor when I told her to take a rinse!'

'That's right,' said Rose, nodding her head up and down, slowly. 'And then you slipped on it and sprained your ankle. You were off work for a week!'

There was a sharp knock on the dentist's door and a squeaky voice shouted: 'Is there anybody in?'

Without waiting for a reply, Grandma opened the door and stuck her head into the room. 'I've come for m' new teeth,' she hissed. 'I hope you've got them ready for me!'

'Mrs Duckworth,' gushed the dentist, rising from his seat, 'how lovely to see you again!'

'Let's get on with it,' snapped Grandma, moving further into the surgery. 'You know I don't like dentists!'

Dudley followed her in and closed the door. He raised his hands and shrugged his shoulders as if to say: 'Sorry!'

'Here, take hold of my bag and my umbrella,' said Grandma, passing the items to Dudley. 'Don't let me go without them.'

Dudley looked ridiculous as he clutched hold of a large shopping bag and a bright red umbrella.

'Well, what are you waiting for?' asked Grandma, glaring at the startled dentist.

'Yes…. right…. er, thank you,' mumbled Mr Brace. He was already a nervous wreck.

Rose took control. 'Come and lie back in the dentist's chair,' she said, putting a firm, guiding hand on Grandma's arm. 'Mr Brace will see to you right away.'

Grandma's eyes lit up. She remembered that chair from her last visit. She hitched up her skirt and slid back on the smooth leather seat. Her hand reached down for the lever immediately.

'It's not quite right,' she said, chewing her gums. 'I'll just adjust it, should I?'

'I'll see to it,' said Rose and she pressed hard on the lever so that Grandma shot backwards in the chair. 'Don't you worry about a thing.'

Both Dudley and Mr Brace gave a satisfied grin.

Rose placed a pair of safety glasses over Grandma's eyes and she positioned a plastic apron across her chest.

'I'm not in for an operation!' snapped Grandma. 'I'm only getting m' false teeth fitted!'

Rose ignored her. She walked across to a cupboard and took out a white plastic box that contained Grandma's new teeth. 'There you are, Mr Brace,' she said, handing over the box. 'The patient is all yours!'

The dentist was feeling more confident. Grandma was so far back in the chair that she couldn't move. Mr Brace put his mask on, leaned over her and said: 'Open wide, please!'

'I can see right up your nose!' said Grandma, suddenly. 'Do you know you've got hairs up your nose, young man? You want to do something about that!'

Dudley cringed with embarrassment as Grandma opened her mouth wide and waited for the startled dentist to make his next move.

## Chapter 3
## On the Bus

'I'm not sure they fit properly,' groaned Grandma, poking a bony finger into her mouth. 'That man seemed in an awful hurry to get me out of there. They feel too loose!'

'They'll be fine,' lied Dudley, as they waited at the bus stop. In truth, he was aware that Grandma's teeth moved up and down freely and clicked every time she spoke. 'You'll just have to wait for them to settle in.'

'I want to go home now,' grumbled Grandma. 'I'm getting cold. M' teeth are chattering.'

Grandma was always either too hot or too cold; she was never just right. Dudley stared down the road and his heart leapt with relief when he saw a red double-decker bus in the distance.

'There's a bus coming,' he said, rubbing his hands together. 'You'll be home in no time, Grandma.' And then Dudley's mouth dropped open in surprise as the half-empty bus picked up speed and raced past the stop.

The bus driver had recognised Grandma and there was no way he was going to let her back on his bus. He remembered her last journey when she had attacked an old man with her umbrella.

'It was self defence!' Grandma had pleaded. 'He kept giving me funny looks!'

It was only when she was thrown off the bus that Grandma realised the old man was blind.

Grandma stared in disbelief after the disappearing bus. 'What did he do that for?' she shouted, waving her bright red umbrella in the air. 'Why did he drive past? There were plenty of places on that bus. He must have seen us waiting!'

'Never mind,' said Dudley, 'there'll be another one along soon.'

They had more luck with the next bus.

Grandma insisted on sitting on the top deck even though Dudley had to give her a shove up the stairs.

'I like to see what's going on,' explained Grandma in a loud voice. 'You can see so much more from the top deck.' She clicked her teeth and settled down into her seat, placing her bag on her knees.

Dudley looked around the bus in embarrassment. He was hoping there was no one on board who would recognise him. However, he was out of luck. Mrs Littler, Dudley's teacher, was sitting a few seats in front on the opposite side of the bus. She was busy marking some books, her brown briefcase open at her feet. Dudley just knew that Grandma would say something.

'Isn't that your teacher?' said Grandma, staring over the top of her seat. 'Mrs Stickler, or whatever she's called?'

It was such a loud whisper that Mrs Littler's ears twitched immediately.

Recognising Grandma's voice, the teacher slid a little further down into her seat.

'It's Mrs *Littler*,' corrected Dudley, grateful that it was half-term. 'Her name's Mrs *Littler*.'

'That's what I said!' snapped Grandma. 'Dreadful woman! I used to know her mother!'

Dudley put his hands over his eyes and wished the world would swallow him up.

A group of youths wearing hooded tops

got on the bus at the next stop. They charged up the stairs and stumbled along the aisle shouting and jeering. Two of them flopped into the seat immediately in front of Dudley and Grandma. Dudley recognised a couple of them.

There was Baz and his dopey friend Roscoe. Baz was a real nuisance who lived in the next street to Dudley. He had greasy black hair and a spotty face and he was always causing trouble.

Grandma glared at them.

Baz shoved a piece of chewing gum into his mouth and immediately started banging on the window and pulling faces at someone on the pavement below. Roscoe chortled with laughter. He thought it was hilarious!

It was too much for Grandma. She tapped Baz on the shoulder with her umbrella and said: 'Excuse me, young man, would you mind sitting quietly?'

Baz turned round and his friends waited for him to react.

'What's up, Grandma?' said Baz, grinning at his friends. 'We're only having a bit of fun.'

'A bit of fun,' repeated Grandma, clicking her teeth. 'You're disturbing other passengers.' She pointed across the bus.

'That's my Dudley's teacher over there. She's trying to mark her school books.'

Mrs Littler slid even further down her seat. She wished she was invisible.

*That's my Dudley's teacher....'* mocked Baz, in a sing-song voice. 'I hate teachers! I was expelled from school, myself!'

'Well, I can't say I'm surprised about that!' snapped Grandma.

'It's all right,' said Dudley, stepping in quickly. He was afraid the situation would get out of control. 'Take no notice of Grandma, she's just a little bit stressed today.'

'Yeah, well she should mind her own business,' grunted Baz and his friends nodded in agreement as Baz settled back into his seat.

'Don't say anything else,' warned Dudley, keeping his voice low. 'They could cause trouble.'

Grandma sucked her teeth, folded her arms and frowned.

A few minutes later, Grandma's nose began to twitch. Dudley looked horrified.

Grandma had the loudest, most violent sneeze in the world and a twitching nose was the first sign.

'No, Grandma!' pleaded Dudley. 'Hold it in! Please hold it in!'

It was too late. Just as the bus was pulling in to a stop, Grandma's head jerked backwards and then shot forward as she let out a most enormous, wet sneeze. The explosion echoed around the top deck of the bus like a whirlwind. Baz let out a startled yell as he felt a damp patch on the back of his head. Mrs Littler shot up from her seat in horror and disappeared down the stairs.

'What on earth was that?' yelled Baz, wiping the back of his head with his hand.

'What was that horrible noise?'

'I'm ... I'm sorry,' muttered Dudley, as
Grandma's nose twitched again. 'She can't
help it! I think she's got an allergy!'

'Let's get out of here!' yelled Baz, signalling to his friends. 'She wants locking up, your grandma! She shouldn't be allowed on public transport!'

The startled youths pushed past and stumbled down the stairs as another violent explosion shook the bus and spattered the windows.

## Chapter 4
## Off to School

Grandma sat up straight, shook her head and wiped her nose with the back of her hand.

It was then that she realised something was wrong. She turned towards her grandson and, in a voice that was trembling with distress, she announced:

'Dudley – I've lost m' new teeth! They must have flown out of my mouth when I sneezed!'

Dudley clasped a hand to his forehead. 'I don't believe it!' he said, slowly. 'You've only just collected them from the dentist!'

'It's not my fault,' said Grandma, pathetically and she smacked her gums together as if in confirmation.

'Well, they can't have gone far,' said Dudley, springing in to action. 'They must be on the floor. Let's take a look underneath the seat before the bus sets off again.'

Downstairs, the driver had no intention of setting off. Startled by Grandma's sneeze, he had watched in surprise as his passengers abandoned the bus. Clearly, someone was causing trouble. He would have to sort it out. The driver left his seat and climbed the stairs, determined to solve the problem.

To his surprise, when he arrived on the top deck, the bus seemed empty. He was just about to turn around and go back down when he heard a grunt and a splutter. It was then that he saw it. Grandma's bottom was sticking up between the seats somewhere around the middle of the bus. There was another grunt and the bottom moved from side to side.

The startled driver advanced cautiously along the aisle until he drew level with the offending object. Grandma was in a most peculiar position, bent double in her seat with her bottom sticking up into the air. She spotted the driver's feet and glanced slowly upwards.

'Hello,' she said, forcing a smile. 'Can you help me, please – I seem to be stuck!'

The driver could not believe his eyes. He crouched down so that he drew level with Grandma's wrinkled face.

'Madam, what on earth are you doing?' he said. 'Have you lost your mind?'

'No, I've lost m' teeth!' replied Grandma. 'You can't see them anywhere, can you?'

At that moment, Dudley crawled out from beneath a seat on the opposite side of the aisle.

'I can explain...' began Dudley, as the driver's mouth dropped open in astonishment.

**********

Grandma and Dudley stood on the pavement and stared after the bus as it disappeared into the distance.

'I've never been thrown off a bus before,' said Dudley, sadly.

'You get used to it,' replied Grandma. 'It's not the end of the world, is it?'

Grandma sucked her gums and scratched her head, thoughtfully. 'Now listen, Dudley,' she continued, 'there was no sign of my teeth on the floor of that bus so they must be somewhere else, mustn't they?'

'That's brilliant, Grandma,' said Dudley, sarcastically. 'I don't know how you do it!'

'The thing is,' said Grandma, looking puzzled, 'where on earth can they be?'

Dudley turned slowly and stared into Grandma's beady eyes. An awful thought had occurred to him.

'You don't think...' he began. 'No... they couldn't be!'

'What?' said Grandma, getting excited. 'What do you think has happened to my teeth?'

'Well,' said Dudley, slowly, 'Mrs Littler was marking books, wasn't she?'

'Yes, yes,' said Grandma, impatiently. 'What's that got to do with anything?'

'And her brown briefcase was wide open on the floor,' continued Dudley. 'Suppose your new teeth flew out when you sneezed and landed in Mrs Littler's briefcase? She got off seconds later, at the stop opposite school.'

Grandma gulped and stared into space. 'My teeth are on the way to school,' she said, slowly. 'Who would have thought it!'

'There's only one thing for it,' said Dudley, grabbing hold of his Gran's arm.

'Come on, Grandma! We'll have to follow them! We're off to school!'

## Chapter 5
## The Brown Briefcase

'Hold my hand, Dudley,' said Grandma quietly, as they stood outside Mrs Littler's classroom waiting to knock.

'It's all right, Grandma,' replied Dudley, looking surprised, 'I'm not worried. Mrs Littler's quite strict but she's not too fierce.'

'It's me that's worried,' whimpered Grandma. 'I don't like teachers. I've never liked teachers. They're a miserable lot, if you ask me.'

'You just leave it to me,' said Dudley, reassuringly. 'I know Mrs Littler will understand.'

In truth, Dudley wasn't quite sure how he was going to explain that his grandma's false teeth were probably in the teacher's briefcase but he took a deep breath and gave a confident knock on the classroom door. There was no reply. Dudley waited a few seconds and then knocked again.

'Right, that's it,' said Grandma, moving away from the door. 'There's no one in; we'd better go home.'

'We're not going anywhere,' said Dudley and he placed a hand on the latch and pushed open the classroom door. 'Come on, Grandma, we'll wait inside. Mrs Littler's sure to be along soon.'

Dudley entered the classroom and Grandma followed him in, reluctantly.

'Are you sure we should be in here on our own?' asked Grandma, peering around the empty room. 'It doesn't seem right.'

'Grandma, trust me,' said Dudley. 'It's my classroom. There won't be a problem.'

Grandma stared around the room at the bright displays and the groups of coloured tables. It was sixty years since she had last been in a classroom and it seemed so strange.

'We had wooden desks in my day,' said Grandma. 'I always had to sit on my own for some reason. I'm not sure why.'

'I can guess,' muttered Dudley, under his breath.

Dudley strolled across to the teacher's desk. 'Look, Grandma,' he said pointing, 'there's a fresh cup of coffee on Mrs Littler's desk. She can't be far away.'

And then he saw it. There, by the side of the teacher's chair, was Mrs Littler's brown briefcase. Dudley moved forward and stared down at it in temptation. He licked his lips, glanced round and said: 'What do you think, Grandma?'

'It wouldn't do any harm, would it?' replied Grandma, in a hoarse whisper. She crept forward and joined Dudley by the brown briefcase. 'I mean, it's not as if we're stealing anything that isn't ours to take – and it would save explaining everything to Mrs Littler.'

'Let's go for it!' said Dudley and he bent down and flicked open the clasp of Mrs Littler's brown briefcase. The lock clicked and the briefcase fell open immediately.

At that very moment, the classroom door opened and Mrs Littler walked into the room. She saw the two figures at once and froze in startled shock. Grandma and Dudley froze, too, so that the people in the room looked like three stone statues.

Grandma was the first to speak. 'I – I can explain,' she stammered, as the teacher rubbed her eyes in disbelief. 'It's – it's not as it seems. Well, it is, actually. Dudley's opened your briefcase and he's looking inside!'

Dudley couldn't believe she'd just said that; it wasn't a good start.

The teacher suddenly exploded into life.

'Dudley Duckworth!' she stormed,

moving forward threateningly. 'What are you doing in my classroom with this awful woman? And why are you rummaging in my briefcase?'

'I'm not that awful!' protested Grandma, looking offended. 'In fact, I'm quite nice when you get to know me!'

Dudley stood up to face the angry teacher. He had a guilty look on his face and he felt ashamed.

'I'm sorry, Mrs Littler,' he began, 'I didn't mean any harm. I was just looking for Grandma's teeth.'

'Don't be ridiculous!' shouted Mrs Littler. She was beginning to lose her temper. 'I've heard some feeble excuses in my time but that beats the lot!'

'He's telling the truth,' interrupted
Grandma. 'Do you remember when I sneezed
on the bus?'

'How could I forget!' said Mrs Littler, screwing up her face.

'Well, m' teeth flew out,' continued Grandma, 'and I think they might have landed in your briefcase. Look, I'll show you.' And Grandma opened her mouth wide to display her floppy pink gums.

'Yes, yes,  all right,' said Mrs Littler, turning away in disgust. 'I suppose it's possible – but you shouldn't have opened my briefcase, should you, Dudley?'

'I'm sorry,' said Dudley, sincerely, 'but I thought you might have got a shock if you put your hand in and pulled out a set of false teeth.'

'Go ahead, then,' agreed Mrs Littler,

shivering at the thought. 'See if your grandma's teeth are in my briefcase.'

'Thanks very much,' said Dudley, reaching forward. 'I knew you'd understand.'

## Chapter 6
## The Hooded Top

'Where on earth can they be?' said
Dudley, as they left the classroom and made
their way down the long corridor. 'I was sure
we'd find them in Mrs Littler's briefcase.'

'They weren't on the floor of the bus
and they weren't in Mrs Littler's briefcase,'

said Grandma, thoughtfully. 'They can't have just vanished into thin air!'

Grandma and Dudley left the school by a side entrance and started to cut across the playground. They heard the noise almost immediately, a strange whooping and screeching sound that seemed to be coming from around the side of the playground.

'It's probably one of the school classes playing out,' said Grandma. 'I love to hear children playing.'

'Grandma, it's half term,' reminded Dudley. 'There are no children in school. Come on, we'd better take a look.'

They rounded the corner and stopped dead in their tracks. Grandma recognised the youths at once, especially Baz, who was leaping around like a monkey, while his friends made strange jungle noises. Baz had a can of spray paint in his hand, which he had obviously already used on the school wall, for there in big blue letters were the words:

Baz's dopey friend Roscoe spotted the two onlookers and pointed in their direction.

'Well, look who it is!' said Baz, swaggering towards Grandma and Dudley.

'My favourite old lady and her silly little grandson!'

'He's not that little!' snapped Grandma, sucking her gums loudly.

'Thanks, Grandma,' said Dudley. 'I really appreciate that!'

'What are you doing in school, you swot?' continued Baz. 'It's half term, isn't it?'

Dudlley thought about telling him the truth for one brief moment but it sounded too ridiculous.

'We needed to see Mrs Littler,' replied Dudley, truthfully, 'but more to the point – what are you doing here?'

'A bit of extra art work,' sniggered Baz, waving the spray can in the air. 'Not that it's any of your business.'

His friends chuckled and nudged each other.

'Baz is really good at art,' chipped in Roscoe. 'It's his favourite subject.'

Dudley noticed that Grandma had gone very quiet. She was just staring at Baz with a strange glint in her eye.

'Are you all right, Grandma?' he said, in a low voice.

'His top,' whispered Grandma. 'He's wearing a hooded top!'

Dudley was worried. Grandma was rambling. Perhaps the stress had been too much for her.

'He's wearing a hooded top,' repeated Grandma, 'and he was sitting directly in front of us on the bus!'

Even Baz was looking concerned. 'You'd better get her home,' he said. 'I think she needs some attention.'

The very next moment, Grandma leapt forward with a yell. She was swinging her bag and waving her red umbrella in the air. Baz was so shocked that he didn't move.

With one vicious swipe, she knocked the can of spray paint from Baz's hand, dropped her umbrella and grabbed hold of Baz's hooded top.

'Get her off! Get her off!' yelled Baz. He was squirming and trying to pull away. 'She's stark raving mad! Get her off!'

His friends took one look at the situation and then turned and ran off as fast as they could.

Suddenly, a loud whistle sounded and Mrs Littler appeared from around the corner, a burly policeman at her side. She had witnessed the vandals spraying the school wall from her classroom window and she had phoned the police.

'That's quite enough!' yelled the policeman, moving in to separate Grandma and Baz. 'You should be ashamed of yourselves!'

'She started it!' yelled Baz, rubbing the back of his head. 'She needs locking up, that old lady! She's ripped my new hooded top!'

Dudley could not believe his eyes. His grandma had gone berserk and now she was in trouble with the police!

'It was a waste of time,' gasped grandma, looking disappointed. 'They weren't there!'

'Madam, what are you talking about?' asked the puzzled policeman, taking hold of Grandma's arm.

'M' teeth, of course,' said Grandma, as if it was obvious, 'they flew out when I sneezed on the bus and that great lout was sitting in front of me. I thought they might have landed in his hood but it was a waste of time.'

'I think you'd better come with me down to the station,' said the policeman and he led Grandma away towards the waiting police car.

## Chapter 7
## Two Sets of Teeth

'I knew he'd understand,' said Grandma, as she waved goodbye to the police car that was pulling away from Dudley's front drive. 'What an adventure, eh, Dudley?'

'Grandma, you've been taken to the police station, questioned for two hours and warned about your future behaviour!' said Dudley, opening the front door. 'I'd hardly call that an adventure!'

'I won't have any of it,' said Grandma, pushing past Dudley into the hallway and placing her umbrella in the stand. 'He was a very nice man and I think he took quite a shine to me.'

'Anyway, the fact remains,' said Dudley, moving into the kitchen, 'we haven't found your teeth. What are we going to do about it, Grandma?'

Grandma placed her bag on the kitchen table and pulled up a chair. She scratched her head and sucked her gums as she considered the situation. Eventually, she said:

'I can't do without m' teeth, Dudley. What am I going to have for my dinner?'

'How about a bowl of custard?' suggested Dudley, quickly. 'Or a nice cup of tomato soup?'

'Don't be ridiculous,' snapped Grandma, scowling. 'You know I don't like custard and I dribble whenever I have soup. No, there's only one thing for it, Dudley – you'll have to take me back to the dentist first thing tomorrow morning.'

Dudley's mouth dropped open and a look of panic crept across his face.

'Back to the dentist,' he repeated, slowly. 'Did you say – back to the dentist?'

'That's right,' said Grandma, and she nodded her head up and down. 'You don't mind, do you, Dudley?' I've got his number here in my bag. You can give him a ring for me.'

Grandma reached across the table for her bag and she thrust her hand inside in search of the dentist's card. She fished around for a moment and then she froze.

Her bottom lip quivered and then her mouth dropped open in surprise.

With sudden realisation, Dudley knew what was about to happen. Ever so slowly,

Grandma withdrew her hand from the bag and there, sitting neatly in between her wrinkled fingers, were a set of false teeth.

Neither Dudley nor Grandma spoke for a few seconds. They just stared down at the gleaming white teeth.

'Well, how about that!' exclaimed Grandma, her face breaking into a gummy smile. 'They were in my bag all the time! What a stroke of luck!'

'I don't believe it!' muttered Dudley. 'They've caused all that trouble and they were in your bag all the time!'

'We should have guessed,' said Grandma, giving her teeth a shake and then popping them straight back into her mouth. 'I was sitting on the bus with my bag on my knee. They must have dropped straight in.'

'Oh, well,' said Dudley, with a resigned sigh. 'All's well that ends well!'

'Ooh, I'm feeling a little bit hungry now that I've got my teeth back,' said Grandma. 'How about making us both a nice cheese and pickle sandwich, Dudley? I'll have a look at the newspaper while you get it ready, should I?' And she shuffled off into the lounge, picking up the paper on the way.

Dudley glared after her but decided to say nothing. After all, he was a little bit peckish himself.

He took two small plates from the kitchen cupboard and then opened the fridge door. Dudley peered inside and then leapt back in horror, for there, on the top shelf of the refrigerator, was a set of false teeth in a glass of water.

'Incredible!' he muttered out loud, when he had stopped shaking. 'She must have put them in the fridge after breakfast!'

'DUDLEY!' shouted Grandma, from the depths of the lounge. 'DUDLEY! Have you seen my glasses anywhere? You'll have to take me to the opticians tomorrow if we don't find them!'

Dudley fell forward, kicked his legs in the air and banged his fists on the kitchen floor.

*Also available in the Reluctant Reader Series*

**Chip McGraw**  *(Cowboy Mystery)*
Ian MacDonald  ISBN 978 1 905637 08 9

**Close Call**  *(Mystery - Interest age 12+)*
Sandra Glover  ISBN 978 1 905 637 07 2

**Beastly Things in the Barn**  *(Humorous)*
Sandra Glover  ISBN 978 1 904904 96 0
www.sandraglover.co.uk

**Cracking Up**  *(Humorous)*
Sandra Glover  ISBN 978 1 904904 86 1

**The Owlers**  *(Adventure)*
Stephanie Baudet  ISBN 978 1 904904 87 8

**Eyeball Soup**  *(Science Fiction)*
Ian MacDonald  ISBN 978 1 904904 59 5

**The Curse of the Full Moon**  *(Mystery)*
Stephanie Baudet  ISBN 978 1 904904 11 3

**The Haunted Windmill**  *(Mystery)*
Margaret Nash  ISBN 978 1 904904 22 9

**Trevor's Trousers**  *(Humorous)*
David Webb  ISBN 978 1 904904 19

**Deadline**  *(Adventure)*
Sandra Glover  ISBN 978 1 904904 30 4

**The Library Ghost**  *(Mystery)*
David Webb  ISBN 978 1 904374 66

**Dinosaur Day**  *(Adventure)*
David Webb  ISBN 978 1 904374 67 1

PUBLISHING

www.eprint.co.uk